GENERAL IRONFIST

BY

ROBERT E. HOWARD

British Library Cataloguing-in-Publication Data
A catalogue record for this book is available from the
British Library

Robert E. Howard

Robert Ervin Howard was born in Peaster, Texas in 1906. During his youth, his family moved between a variety of Texan boomtowns, and Howard – a bookish and somewhat introverted child – was steeped in the violent myths and legends of the Old South. Although he loved reading and learning, Howard developed a distinctly Texan, hardboiled outlook on the world. He became a passionate fan of boxing, taking it up at an amateur level, and from the age of nine began to write adventure tales of semi-historical bloodshed. In 1919, when Howard was thirteen, his family moved to the Central Texas hamlet of Cross Plains, where he would stay for the rest of his life.

At fifteen Howard began to read the pulp magazines of the day, and to write more seriously. The December 1922 issue of his high school newspaper featured two of his stories, 'Golden Hope Christmas' and 'West is West'. In 1924 he sold his first piece – a short caveman tale titled 'Spear and Fang' – for $16 to the not-yet-famous *Weird Tales* magazine. He published with the magazine regularly over the next few years. 1929 was a breakout year for Howard, in that the 23-year-old writer began to sell to other magazines, such as *Ghost Stories* and *Argosy*, both of whom had previously sent him hundreds of rejection slips. In 1930, he began a correspondence with weird fiction master H. P. Lovecraft which ran up to his death six years later, and is regarded as one of the great correspondence cycles in all of fantasy literature.

It was partly due to Lovecraft's encouragement that Howard created his most famous character, Conan the Cimmerian. Conan – a barbarian-turned-King during the Hyborian Age, a mythical period of some 12,000 years ago – featured in seventeen *Weird Tales* stories between 1933 and 1936, and is now regarded as having spawned the 'sword and sorcery' genre, making Howard's influence on fantasy literature comparable to that of J. R. R. Tolkien's. The Conan stories have since been adapted many times, most famously in the series of films starring Arnold Schwarzenegger.

Howard was enjoying an all-time high in sales by the beginning of 1936, but he was also deeply upset by the ill health of his mother, who had fallen into a coma. On the morning of June 11, 1936, he asked an attending nurse whether she would ever recover, and the nurse replied negatively. Howard walked to his car, parked outside the family home in Cross Plains, and shot himself. He died eight hours later, aged just thirty.

AS I CLUMB into the ring that night in the Pleasure Palace Fight Club, on the Hong Kong waterfront, I was low in my mind. I'd come to Hong Kong looking for a former shipmate of mine. I'd come on from Tainan as fast as I could, even leaving my bulldog Mike aboard the *Sea Girl*, which wasn't due to touch at Hong Kong for a couple of weeks yet.

But Soapy Jackson, the feller I was looking for, had just dropped plumb out of sight. Nobody'd saw him for weeks, or knowed what had become of him. Meanwhile my dough was all gone, so I accepted a bout with a big Chinese fighter they called the Yeller Typhoon.

He was a favorite with the sporting crowd and the Palace was jammed with both white men and Chineses that night, some very high class. I noticed one Chinee in particular, whilst setting in my corner waiting for the bell, because his European clothes was so swell, and because he seemed to take such a burning interest in the goings on. But I didn't pay much attention to the crowd; I was impatient to get the battle over with.

The Yeller Typhoon weighed three hundred pounds and he was a head taller'n me; but most of his weight was around his waist-line, and he didn't have the kind of arms and shoulders that makes a hitter. And it don't make no difference how big a Chinaman is, he can't take it.

3

I wasn't in no mood for classy boxing that night. I just walked into him, let him flail away with both hands till I seen a opening, and then let go my right. He shook the ring when he hit the boards, and the brawl was over.

Paying no heed to the howls of the dumbfounded multitude, I hastened to my dressing-room, donned my duds, and then hauled a letter from my britches pocket and studied it like I'd done a hundred times before.

It was addressed to Mr. Soapy Jackson, American Bar, Tainan, Taiwan, and was from a San Francisco law firm. After Soapy left the *Sea Girl*, he tended bar at the American, but he'd been gone a month when the *Sea Girl* docked at Tainan again, and the proprietor showed me that letter which had just come for him. He said Soapy had went to Hong Kong, but he didn't know his address, so I took the letter and come on alone to find him, because I had a idea it was important. Maybe he'd been left a fortune.

But I'd found Hong Kong in turmoil, just like all the rest of China. Up in the hills a lot of bandits, which called themselves revolutionary armies, was raising hell, and all I couldst hear was talk about General Yun Chei, and General Whang Shan, and General Feng, which they said was really a white man. Folks said Yun and Feng had joined up against Whang, and some tall battling was expected, and the foreigners was all piling down out of the interior. It was easy for a white sailorman with no connections to drop out of sight and never be heard of again. I thought what if Soapy has got hisself scuppered by them bloody devils, just when maybe he was on the p'int of coming into big money.

Well, I stuck the letter in my pocket, and sallied forth into the lamp-lit street to look for Soapy some more, when somebody hove up alongside of me, and who should it be but that dapper Chinee in European clothes I'd noticed in the first row, ringside, at the fight.

"You are Sailor Costigan, are you not?" he said in perfect English.

"Yeah," I said, after due consideration.

"I saw you fight the Yellow Typhoon tonight," he said. "The blow you dealt him would have felled an ox. Can you always hit like that?"

"Why not?" I inquired. He looked me over closely, and nodded his head like he was agreeing with hisself about something.

"Come in and have a drink," he said, so I follered him into a native joint where they wasn't nothing but Chineses. They looked at me with about as much expression as fishes, and went on guzzling tea and rice wine out of them little fool egg-shell cups. The mandarin, or whatever he was, led the way into a room which the door was covered with velvet curtains and the walls had silk hangings with dragons all over 'em, and we sot down at a ebony table and a Chinaboy brung in a porcelain jug and the glasses.

The mandarin poured out the licker, and, whilst he was pouring mine, such a infernal racket arose outside the door that I turned around and looked, but couldn't see nothing for the curtains, and the noise quieted down all of a sudden. Them Chineses is always squabbling amongst theirselves.

So the mandarin said, "Let us drink to your vivid victory!"

"Aw," I said, "that wasn't nothin'. All I had to do was hit him."

But I drank, and I said, "This is funny tastin' stuff. What is it?"

"*Kaoliang*," he said. "Have another glass." So he poured 'em, and nigh upsot my glass with his sleeve as he handed it to me.

So I drank it, and he said, "What's the matter with your ears?"

"You oughta know, bein' a fight fan," I said.

"This fight tonight was the first I have ever witnessed," he confessed.

"I'd never thought it from the interest you've taken in the brawl," I said. "Well, these ears is what is known in the vernacular of the game as cauliflowers. I got 'em, also this undulatin' nose, from stoppin' gloves with human knuckles inside of 'em. All old-timers is similarly decorated, unless they happen to be of the dancin'-school variety."

"You have fought in the ring many times?" he inquired.

"Oftener'n I can remember," I answered, and his black eyes gleamed with some secret pleasure. I took another snort of that there Chinese licker out of the jug, and I begun to feel oratorical and histrionic.

"From Savannah to Singapore," I said, "from the alleys of Bristol to the wharfs of Melbourne, I've soaked the resin dust with my blood and the gore of my enemies. I'm the bully of the *Sea Girl*, the toughest ship afloat, and when I set foot on the docks, strong men hunt cover! I—"

I suddenly noticed my tongue was getting thick and my head was swimming. The mandarin wasn't making no attempt to talk. He was setting staring at me kinda intense-like, and his eyes glittered through a mist which was beginning to float about me.

"What the heck!" I said stupidly. Then I heaved up with a roar, and the room reeled around me. "You yeller-bellied bilge-rat!" I roared drunkenly. "You done doped my grog! You—"

I grabbed him by the shirt with my left, and dragged him across the table top, drawing back my right, but before I could bash him with it, something exploded at the base of my skull, and the lights went out.

I MUST OF been out a long time. Once or twice I had a sensation of being tossed and jounced around, and thought I was in my bunk and a rough sea running, and then again I kinda vaguely realized that I was bumping over a rutty road in a automobile, and I had a feeling that I ought to get up and knock somebody's block off. But mostly I just laid there and didn't know nothing at all.

When I did finally come to myself, the first thing I discovered was that my hands and feet was tied with ropes. Then I seen I was laying on a camp cot in a tent, and a big Chinaman with a rifle was standing over me. I craned my neck, and seen another man setting on a pile of silk cushions, and he looked kinda familiar.

At first I didn't recognize him, because now he was dressed in embroidered silk robes, Chinese style, but then I seen it was the mandarin. I struggled up to a sitting position, in spite of my bonds, and addressed him with poignancy and fervor.

"Why," I concluded passionately, "did you dope my licker? Where am I at? What've you done with me, you scum of a Macao gutter?"

"You are in the camp of General Yun Chei," he said. "I transported you hither in my automobile while you lay senseless."

"And who the devil are you?" I demanded.

He gave me a sardonic bow. "I am General Yun Chei, your humble servant," he said.

"The hell you are!" I commented with a touch of old-world culture. "You had a nerve, comin' right into Hong Kong."

"The Federalist fools are blind," he said. "Often I play my own spy."

"But what'd you kidnap *me* for?" I yelled with passion, jerking at my cords till the veins stood out on my temples. "I can't pay no cussed ransom."

"Have you ever heard of General Feng?" he asked.

"And what if I has?" I snarled, being in no mood for riddles.

"He is camped nearby," said he. "He is a white foreign-devil like yourself. You have heard his nickname—?"

"Well?" I demanded.

"He is a man of great strength and violent passions," said General Yun. "He has acquired a following more because of his personal fighting ability than because of his intellect. Whomever he strikes with his fists falls senseless to the ground. So the soldiers call him .

"Now, he and I have temporarily allied our forces, because our mutual enemy, General Whang Shan, is somewhere in the vicinity. General Whang has a force greater than ours, and he likewise possesses an airplane, which he flies himself. We do not know exactly where he is, but, on the other hand, he does not know our position, either, and we are careful to guard against spies. No one leaves or enters our camp without special permission.

"Though and myself are temporary allies, there is no love lost between us, and he constantly seeks to undermine my prestige with my men. To protect myself I must retaliate— not so as to precipitate trouble between our armies, but in such a way as to make him lose face.

"General Feng boasts that he can conquer any man in China with his naked fists, and he has frequently dared me to pit my hardiest captains against him for the sheer sport of it. He well knows that no man in my army could stand up against him, and his arrogance lowers my prestige. So I went secretly to Hong Kong to find a man who might have a fighting chance against him. I contemplated the Yellow Typhoon, but when you laid him low with a single stroke, I knew you were the man for whom I was looking. I have many friends in Hong Kong. Drugging you was easy. The first time a pre-arranged noise at the door distracted your attention. But that was not enough, so I contrived to dope your second drink under cover of my sleeve. By the holy dragon, you had enough drug in you to have overcome an elephant before you succumbed!

"But here you are. I shall present you to General Feng, before all the captains, and challenge him to make good his boast. He cannot with honor refuse; and if you beat him, he will lose face, and my prestige will rise accordingly, because you represent me."

"And what do I get out of it?" I demanded.

"If you win," he said, "I will send you back to Hong Kong with a thousand American dollars."

"And what if I lose?" I said.

"Ah," he smiled bleakly, "a man whose head has been removed by the executioner's sword has no need of money."

I burst into a cold sweat and sot in silent meditation.

"Do you agree?" he asked at last.

"I'd like to know what choice I got," I snarled. "Take these here cords offa me and gimme some grub. I won't fight for nobody on a empty belly."

He clapped his hands, and the soldier cut my cords with his bayonet, and another menial come in with a big dish of mutton stew and some bread and rice wine, so I fell to and lapped it all up in a hurry.

"As a token of appreciation," said General Yun, "I now make you a present of this unworthy trinket."

And he hauled out the finest watch I ever seen and give it to me.

"If the gift pleases you," he said, noting my gratification, "let it nerve your thews against ."

"Don't worry about that," I said, admiring the watch, which was gold with dragons carved on it. "I'll bust him so hard he'll be loopin' the loop for a week."

"Excellent!" beamed General Yun. "If you could contrive to deal him a fatal injury during the combat, it could simplify matters greatly. But come! I shall tangle General Feng in his own web!"

I FOLLERED HIM out of the tent, and seen a lot of other tents and ragged soldiers drilling amongst 'em, and off to one side another camp with more yeller-bellied gunmen in it. It was still kinda early in the morning, and I gathered it had tooken us all night to get there in Yun's auto. We was away up in the hills, and they was no sign of civilization anywheres.

General Yun headed straight for a big tent in the middle of the camp, and I follered him in. A lot of officers in all kinds of uniforms riz and bowed, except one big man who sot on a camp stool. He was a white man in faded khaki and boots and a sun helmet; his fists was as big as mauls, and his hairy arms was thick with muscles. His face and corded neck was burned brick-colored by the sun, and he wore a expression like he habitually hankered for somebody to give him a excuse to slug 'em.

"General Yun—" he begun in a harsh voice, then stopped and glared at me. "What the hell are you doing here?" he demanded.

"Joel Ballerin!" I said, staring at him. I might of knowed. Wherever they was war, you'd usually find Joel Ballerin right in the middle of it. He was from South Australia, and had a natural instinct for carnage. He was famed as a fighting man all over South Africa, Australia and the South Seas. Gunrunner, blackbirder, smuggler, pirate, pearler, or what have you, but always a scrapper from the word go, with a constant hankering to bounce his enormous fists offa somebody's conk. I'd never fit him, but I'd saw some of his handiwork. The ruin he could make of a human carcass was plumb appalling.

He glared at me with no love, because I got considerable reputation as a man-mauler myself, and fighting men is jealous of each other's fame. I couldst feel my own short hairs bristle as I glared at him.

"You have boasted much of your prowess with the clenched fist," said Yun Chei, softly. "You have repeatedly assured me that there was not a man in my army, including my unworthy self, whom you could not subdue with ease. I have here one of my followers whom I venture to back against you."

"That's Steve Costigan, an American sailor," snarled Ballerin. "He's no man of yours."

"On the contrary!" said General Yun. "Do you not see that he wears my dragon watch, entrusted only to my loyal henchmen?"

"Well," growled Ballerin, "there's something fishy about this. When you bring that cabbage-eared gorilla up here—"

"Hey!" I said indignantly. "You cease heavin' them insults around! If you ain't got the guts to fight, why, say so!"

"Why, you blasted fool!" he roared, jumping up off his stool like it was red hot. "I'll break your infernal head right here and now—"

General Yun got between us and smiled blandly and said, "Let us be dignified in all things. Let it be a public exhibition. I fear this tent would not prove a proper arena for two such gladiators. I shall have a ring constructed at once."

Ballerin turned away, grunting, "All right; fix it any way you want to." Then he wheeled back, his eyes flaming, and snarled at me, "As for you, you Yankee ape, you're going out of this camp feet-first!"

"Big talk don't bust no chins," I retorted. "I never did like you anyway, you nigger-stealin' pearl-thief!"

He looked like he was going to bust some blood-vessels, but he just give a ferocious snarl and plunged out of the tent. General Yun motioned me to foller him, and his officers tagged after us. The others follered General Feng. They didn't seem to be no love lost betwixt them two armies.

" is caught in his own snare!" gurgled General Yun, hugging hisself with glee. "He lusts for battle, but is furious and suspicious because I trapped him into it. All the men of both armies shall see his downfall. Call in the patrols from the hills! General Ironfist! Ha!"

GENERAL YUN DIDN'T take me back to his tent, but he put me in another'n and told me to holler if I wanted anything. He said I'd be guarded so's Ballerin couldn't have me bumped off, but I seen I was as good as a prisoner.

Well, I sot in there, and heard some men come marching up and surround the tent, and somebody give orders in broken Chinese, and cussed heartily in English, and I stuck my head out of the door and hollered, *"Soapy!"*

There he was, all right, commanding the guard, with a old British army coat three sizes too small for him, and a sword three sizes too big. He nigh dropped his sword when he seen me, and bellered, "Steve! What you doin' here?"

"I come up to lick Joel Ballerin for Yun Chei," I said. And he said, "So that's why they're buildin' that ring! Nobody but the highest officers knows what's goin' on."

"What you doin' here?" I demanded.

"Aw," he said, "I got tired tendin' bar and decided to become a soldier of fortune. So I skipped to Hong Kong and beat it up into the hills and joined Yun Chei. But Steve, the life ain't what it's cracked up to be. I don't mind the fightin' much, cause it's mostly yellin' and shootin' and little damage done, but marchin' through these hills is hell, and the food is lousy. We don't get paid regular, and no place to spend the dough when we do get it. For ten cents I'd desert."

"Well, lissen," I said, "I got a letter for you." I reached into my britches pocket, and then I give a yelp. "I been rolled!" I hollered. "It's gone!"

"What?" he said.

"Your letter," I said. "I was lookin' for you to give it to you. It come to the American Bar at Tainan. A letter from the Ormond and Ashley law firm, 'Frisco."

"What was in it?" he demanded.

"How should I know?" I returned irritably. "I didn't open it. I thought maybe somebody had left you a lot of dough, or somethin'."

"I've heard pa say he had wealthy relatives," said Soapy, doubtfully. "Look again, Steve."

"I've looked," I said. "It ain't here. I bet Yun Chei took it offa me whilst I was out. I'll go over and bust him on the jaw—"

"Wait!" hollered Soapy. "You'll get us both shot! You ain't supposed to leave this tent, and I got to guard you."

"Well," I said, "t'aint likely they was any money in the letter. Likely they was just tellin' you where to go to get the dough. I remember the address, and when I get back to Hong Kong, I'll write and tell 'em I got you located."

"That's a long time to wait," said Soapy, pessimistically.

"Not so long," I said. "As soon as I lick Ballerin, I'll start for Hong Kong—"

"No, you won't," said Soapy. "No ways soon, anyhow."

"What d'you mean?" I asked. "Yun said he'd send me back if I licked Ballerin."

"He didn't say when, did he?" inquired Soapy. "He ain't goin' to take no chance of you going back and talkin' and revealin' our position to Whang's spies. No, sir; he'll keep you prisoner till he's ready to change camp, and that may be six months."

"Me stay in this dump six months?" I exclaimed fiercely. "I won't do it!"

"Maybe you won't at that," he said cheeringly. "A lot of things can happen unexpected around a rebel Chinee camp. I see you're wearin' Yun Chei's dragon watch."

"Yeah," I said. "Ain't it a beaut? Yun Chei give it to me."

"Well" he said, "that watch has been give away before, but it has a way of comin' back to Yun Chei after the owner's demise, which is generally sudden and frequent. Four men that I know of has already been made a present of that watch, and none of 'em is now alive."

"The hell you say!" I said, beginning to perspire copiously. "This is a nice, friendly place I got into. Do *you* want to stay here?"

"No, I don't!" he replied bitterly. "I didn't want to before, and when I thinks they's maybe a million dollars waitin' somewhere for me to spend, I feels like throwin' down this fool sword and headin' for the coast."

"Well," I said, "I ain't goin' to spend no six months here. Yet I wants that thousand bucks. Let's us make a break tonight, after I collects."

"They'd run us down before we'd went far," he said despondently. "I got one of the few good horses in camp, but it couldn't carry us both at any kind of a clip. All the other nags are fastened up and guarded so nobody can desert and carry news of our whereabouts to General Whang, which would give a leg to know, so he could raid us. Yun Chei knows he can trust me not to, because Whang wants to cut off my head. I stole a batch of his eatin' chickens onst when we was fightin' him over near Kauchau."

"Well," I begun hotly, "I'll be derned if *I'm* goin' to—"

"Shhh!" he said. "We got to change guard now; here comes the other squad. I'm goin' off somewheres and think."

Another gang of Chinamen come up with a native officer in charge, and Soapy and his men marched off, and I sot and wound my dragon watch, and tried to think of something, but didn't have no success, as usual.

TIME DRAGGED SLOW, but finally about the middle of the afternoon, a mob of captains or something come and led me out of the tent and escorted me to the ring which had been built about halfway between the camps. They was already a solid bank of soldiers around it, Yun Chei's on one side and General Feng's on the other, with their rifles. The ring was just four posts stuck in the ground, with ropes stretched between 'em, and a bare floor of boards elevated maybe a yard or more. General Yun was setting in a camp chair on one side, with his officers around him, and a big Chinee, which was naked to the waist, was standing right behind him. The other officers and the common soldiers of both armies sot on the ground or stood up.

I didn't see Soapy nowheres, and they wasn't no seconds nor handlers. The Chineses didn't know nothing about such things. I clumb into the ring and examined the ropes, which was too loose, for one thing, and the floor, which was solid enough but none too even, and no padding of any kind on it. They had had sense enough to put camp stools in the corners, so I shed my cap, coat and shirt, and sot down. General Yun then riz and come over to me and smiled gently and said, "Smite the dog as you smote the Yellow Typhoon. If you lose the fight, you will lose your head in this very ring."

"I ain't goin' to lose," I snarled, being fed up on that kind of talk, and he smiled benevolently and retired to his chair. Just then somebody yanked my pants leg, and I looked down and seen Soapy. He was shaking with excitement.

"Don't talk, Steve!" he whispered. "Just lissen! Yun Chei thinks I'm encouragin' you for the battle. But lissen:

19

I've fixed it! I got wind of a Federal army camped in a valley to the south. They don't know nothin' about us, but I found a man who swore I could trust him, and I smuggled him off on my horse. He'll guide 'em back here, and they'll break up this den of thieves. When the shootin' starts, we'll duck and run for the Federal lines. I sent my man right after I talked to you this mornin', so they oughta get here in maybe an hour or so."

"Well," I said, "I hope they don't get here too soon; I want to collect my thousand bucks from Yun Chei before I run."

"I'm goin' to snoop amongst Feng's men," he hissed, and just then the crowd on the opposite side of the ring divided, and here come Feng hisself, alias Joel Ballerin.

He was stripped to the waist, and he wore his fighting scowl. His short blond hair bristled, and his men sent up a cheer. He *was* big, and well built for speed and power. He had broad, square shoulders, a big arching chest, and a heavy neck, and his muscles fairly bulged under his sun-reddened skin with every move he made. He stood square on his wide-braced legs, and they showed plenty of power and drive. He was a fraction of a inch taller'n me, and weighed about 200 to my 190, all bone and muscle and hellfire.

Looking back on that fight, it was one of the strangest I ever mixed in. They wasn't no referee. They was a Chinaman who whanged a gong every now and then when he remembered to, but he wasn't no-ways consistent in his time-keeping. Some of the rounds lasted thirty seconds and some lasted nine or ten minutes. When one of us went down, they wasn't no counting. The idea was that we should just keep on battling till one of us wasn't able to get up at all. We hadn't no gloves. Bare knuckles don't jolt like the mitts, but they cut and bruise. It's hard to knock out a tough man in good condition with one lick or half a dozen licks of your bare maulers. You got to plumb butcher him.

They was few preliminaries. Ballerin vaulted into the ring, kicked his stool through the ropes, and yelled, "Hit that gong, Wu Shang!" Wu Shang hit it, and Ballerin come for me like a cross between a bucking bronco and a China typhoon.

We met in the center of the ring like a thunder-clap, and his first lick split my left cauliflower, and my first clout laid his jaw open to the bone. After that it was slaughter and massacre.

There wasn't nothing fancy about our battling. It was toe to toe, and breast to breast, bare knuckles crunching against muscle and bone. Before the first round was over we was slipping in smears of our own blood. In the second Ballerin nearly fractured my jaw with a blazing left hook that stretched me on the floor. But I was up and slugging like mad at the bell. We begun the third by rushing from our corners with such fury that we had a head-on collision which dumped us both to the boards nigh senseless. Ballerin's scalp was laid open, and my head had a bump on it as big as a egg. The Chineses screamed with amazement, seeing us both writhing on the floor, but we staggered up about the same time and begun swinging at each other when Wu Shang got rattled and hit the gong.

AT THE BEGINNING of the fourth I started bombarding Ballerin's mid-section whilst he pounded my head till my ears was ringing like all the ship bells in Frisco harbor, and the blood got in my eyes till I couldn't see and was hitting by instinct. I could hear him gasping and panting as my iron maulers sunk deeper and deeper into his suffering belly, and finally, with a maddened roar, he grappled me and threw me, and, setting astraddle of me, begun pounding my head against the boards, to the great glee of his warriors.

As Wu Shang seemed inclined to let that round go on forever, I resorted to some longshoreman tactics myself, kicked lustily in the back of the head, arched my body and threw him off of me, and pasted him beautifully in the eye as he riz.

This reduced his available sight by half, and didn't improve his temper none, as he proved by giving vent to a screech like a steam whistle, and letting go a hurricane swing that caught me under the ear and wafted me across the ring into the ropes. Them being too loose, I continued my flight unchecked and lit headfirst in the laps of the soldiers outside.

I riz and started to climb back through the ropes, necessarily tromping on my victims as I done so, and one would've stabbed me with his bayonnet by way of reprisal if I hadn't thoughtfully kicked him in the jaw first. Then I seen Ballerin crouching at the ropes, grinning fiercely at me as he dripped blood and weighed his huge fists, and I seen his intention of socking me as I clumb through. I said, "Get back from them ropes and let me in, you scum of the bilge!"

"That's up to you, you wind-jamming baboon!" he laughed brutally. So I unexpectedly reached through the ropes and grabbed his ankle and dumped him on his neck, and before he could rise, I was back in the ring. He riz ravening, and just then Wu Shang decided to hit the gong.

At the beginning of the fifth we came together and slugged till we was blind and deaf and dizzy, and when we finally heard the gong, we dropped in our tracks and lay there side by side, gasping for breath, till the gong announced the opening of the sixth, and we riz up and started in where we'd left off.

We was exchanging lefts and rights like a hail storm when he brung one up from the floor so fast I never seen it coming. The first part of me that hit the boards was the back of my head, and it nigh caved in the floor. I riz and tore into him, slugging with frenzied abandon, and battered him back across the ring, but I was so blind I missed him as he side-stepped, and fell into the ropes, and he smashed me three times behind the ear, and then, as I wheeled groggily, he caught me square on the button with a most awful right swing. *Wham!* I don't remember falling, but I must of, because the next thing I knowed I was down on the boards and Ballerin was stomping in my ribs with his boots. Away off I could hear Wu Shang banging his gong, but Ballerin give no heed, and I felt myself slipping into dreamland.

Then my blood-misted gaze, wandering at random, rested on General Yun in his camp chair. He smiled at me grimly, and that half-naked Chinaman behind him drawed a great curved sword and run his thumb along the edge.

With a howl of desperation I steadied my tottering brain, and I fought my way to my feet in spite of all Ballerin could do, and I pasted him with a left that tore his ear nearly off his head, and he went reeling into the ropes. He come back with a roar and a tremendous clout that missed me and splintered one of the ring posts, and I heaved my right under his heart with all my beef behind it. I heard a couple of his ribs crack under it, and I follered it with a hurricane of lefts and rights that drove him staggering before me like a ship in a typhoon. A thundering right to the head bent him back over the ropes, and then, just as I was setting myself for the finisher, I felt somebody jerking my pants leg and heard

Soapy hollering to me amidst the roar of the mob, "Steve! Ballerin's got fifty rifles trained on you right now. If you drop him, you'll never leave that ring alive."

I SHOOK THE blood outa my eyes and cast a desperate glare over my shoulder. The front ranks of General Feng's warriors still leaned on their rifles, but behind 'em I caught a glimmer of black muzzles.

Ballerin pitched off the ropes, swinging a wild overhand right that missed by a yard, and he would of tumbled to the boards if I hadn't grabbed him and held him up.

"What'm I goin' to do?" I howled. "If I don't drop him, Yun Chei'll cut off my head, and if I do, his men'll shoot me!"

"Stall, Steve!" begged Soapy. "Keep it up as long as you can; somethin' might happen any minute now."

I cast a glance at the sun, and sweated with despair. But I held Ballerin up as long as I dared, and then I pushed him away from me and swung wide at him. He reeled and I tried to catch him, but he pitched face-first, and I ducked as I heard a click of rifle bolts. But he was trying to climb up again, and I never hoped to see a opponent rise like I hoped to see him rise. He grabbed the ropes and hauled hisself up, and stared around, one eye closed and t'other glassy.

He was out on his feet, but his fighting instinct kept him going. He come blundering out into the ring, swinging blind, and I swung wide, but he fell into it somehow, and

I hit him in spite of myself. Soapy give a lamentable howl, and Ballerin pitched back into the ropes, and I was on him and locked him in a despairing grasp before he could fall. He was dead weight in my arms, out cold, his legs dragging, and I was so near out myself I wondered how long I couldst hold him up. Over his shoulder I see General Yun looking at me impatient; even a Chinese revolutionist could see that was ready for the cleaners. But I held on; if I let go, I knowed Ballerin wouldn't get up again, and his men would start target practice on me.

Then above the noise of the crowd I heard a low roar. I looked out over their heads, and beyond the ridge of a distant hill something come soaring. It was a airplane, and nobody but me had seen it. I wrestled my limp victim to the ropes, and gasped the news to Soapy. He was too smart to look, but he hissed, "Keep stallin'! Hold him up! The Federals have sent a plane to our rescue! Everything's jake!"

General Yun had got suspicious. He jumped up and shook his fist at me, and hollered, and his derned executioner grinned and drawed his sword again—and then, with a rush and zoom, the airplane swooped down on us like a hawk. Everybody looked up and yelled, and as it passed right over the ring, I seen something tumble from it and flash in the sun. And Soapy yelled, "Look out! There's a dragon painted on it! That ain't a Federal plane—that's *Whang Shan!*"

I throwed Ballerin bodily over the ropes as far as I could heave him, and div after him, and the next instant— *blam!*—the ring went up in smoke, and pieces flew every which way.

BOMBS WAS FALLING and crashing and tents going sky-high, and men yelling and shooting and running and falling over each other, and the roar of that cussed plane was in my ears as I headed for the tall timber. I was vaguely aware that Soapy was legging it alongside me, hollering, "That Chinaman of mine never went to the Federals, the dirty rat! I see it all now! He was one of Whang Shan's spies. No wonder he was so anxious to help! He wanted my horse—hey, Steve! This way!"

I seen Soapy do a running dive into General Yun's auto, which was setting in front of his tent, and I follered him. We went roaring away just as a bomb hit where the car had been a second before, and spattered us with dirt. I dunno where General Yun was, though I caught a glimpse of a silk-robed figure, which might of been him, scudding for the hills.

We went through that camp like a tornado, with all hell popping behind us. Whang was sure giving his enermies the works in that one plane of his'n. They was such punk shots they couldn't hit him with their rifles, and all he had to do was heave bombs into the thick of 'em.

I don't remember much about that ride. Soapy was hanging to the wheel and pushing the accelerator through the floor, and I was holding onto the seat and trying to stay with the derned craft which was bucking over that awful road like a skiff in a squall. Presently we hit a bump that throwed me clean over the seat into the back, and when I come up for air I had something clutched in my hand, at the sight of which I give a yell of joy—and bit my tongue savagely as we hit another bump.

I clumb back into the front seat like I was crawling along the cross-trees of the main-mast in a typhoon, and tried to tell Soapy what I'd found, but we was going so fast the wind blowed the words clean outa my mouth.

It wasn't till we had dropped down out of the higher hills along about sundown and was coasting along a comparatively better road amongst fields and mud huts that I got a chance to catch my breath.

"I found your letter," I said. "It was in the bottom of the car. It must of slipped outa my pocket whilst I was tied up."

"Read it to me," he requested, and I said, "Wait till I see is my watch intact. I didn't get my thousand bucks for lickin' Ballerin, and I want to be sure I got *somethin*, for goin' through what I been through."

So I looked at the watch, which must of been worth five hundred dollars anyway, and it was unscratched, so I opened the letter and read: "Ormond and Ashley, attorneys at law, San Francisco, California, U. S. A. Dear Mister Jackson: This

is to inform you that you are being sued by Mrs. J. A. Lynch
for a nine months board bill, amounting to exactly—"

Soapy give a ear-splitting yell and wrenched the wheel
over.

"What you doin', you idjit?" I howled, as the car r'ared
and skidded and lurched around like a skiff in a tide-rip.

"I'm goin' back to Yun Chei!" he screeched. "My
expectations is bust! I thought I was a heiress, but I'm still a
bum! I ain't got the—"

Crash! We left the road, rammed a tree, and went into
a perfect tailspin.

The evening shadders was falling as I crawled out from
under the debris and untangled one of the wheels from
around my neck. I looked about for Soapy's remains, and
seen 'em setting on a busted headlight, brooding somberly.

"You might at least ask if I'm hurt," I said resentfully.

"What of it?" he asked bitterly. "We're ruined. I ain't
got not fortune."

"I was ruined when I first met a hoodoo like you," I
said fiercely. "Anyway, I still got Yun Chei's watch." And I
reached into my pocket. And then I gave a poignant shriek.
That watch must of absorbed the whole jolt of the smash. I
had a handful of metal scraps and wheels and springs which
nobody could tell was they meant for a watch or what.
Thereafter, a figure might have been seen flitting through the

twilight, hotly pursued by another, bulkier figure, breathing threats of vengeance, in the general direction of the coast.

THE END